The Best of Poe

Edgar Allan Poe

SADDLEBACK
EDUCATIONAL PUBLISHING

Saddleback's *Illustrated Classics*

SADDLEBACK
EDUCATIONAL PUBLISHING
www.sdlback.com

ISBN-13: 978-1-56254-884-1
ISBN-10: 1-56254-884-0
eBook: 978-1-60291-141-3

Printed in Malaysia

20 19 18 17 16   7 8 9 10 11

Welcome to
Saddleback's *Illustrated Classics*

We are proud to welcome you to Saddleback's *Illustrated Classics*. Saddleback's *Illustrated Classics* was designed specifically for the classroom to introduce readers to many of the great classics in literature. Each text, written and adapted by teachers and researchers, has been edited using the Dale-Chall vocabulary system. In addition, much time and effort has been spent to ensure that these high-interest stories retain all of the excitement, intrigue, and adventure of the original books.

With these graphically *Illustrated Classics*, you learn what happens in the story in a number of different ways. One way is by reading the words a character says. Another way is by looking at the drawings of the character. The artist can tell you what kind of person a character is and what he or she is thinking or feeling.

This series will help you to develop confidence and a sense of accomplishment as you finish each novel. The stories in Saddleback's *Illustrated Classics* are fun to read. And remember, fun motivates!

Overview

Everyone deserves to read the best literature our language has to offe Saddleback's *Illustrated Classics* was designed to acquaint readers wit the most famous stories from the world's greatest authors, while teach ing essential skills. You will learn how to:

- Establish a purpose for reading
- Activate prior knowledge
- Evaluate your reading
- Listen to the language as it is written
- Extend literary and language appreciation through
  discussion and writing activities.

Reading is one of the most important skills you will ever learn. It provide the key to all kinds of information. By reading the *Illustrated Classic* you will develop confidence and the self-satisfaction that comes from accomplishment—a solid foundation for any reader.

Step-By-Step

The following is a simple guide to using and enjoying each of your *Illustrated Classics*. To maximize your use of the learning activities provided, we suggest that you follow these steps:

1. ***Listen!*** We suggest that you listen to the read-along. (At this time, please ignore the beeps.) You will enjoy this wonderfully dramatized presentation.

2. ***Post-reading Activities.*** You have successfully read the story and listened to the audio presentation. Now answer the multiple-choice questions and other activities in the Study Guide.

Remember,

"Today's readers are tomorrow's leaders."

Edgar Allan Poe

Edgar Allan Poe was born in Boston in 1809 and is considered to be one of the most famous figures in American literary history. His works included poetry, literary criticisms, as well as short stories. He is known for writings that were morbid and bizarre.

His father and mother were traveling actors. Poe was orphaned at the age of two. He became the ward of John Allan, a Richmond merchant. John Allan supported Poe when he enrolled at the University of Virginia. But Poe was addicted to gambling and ran up huge gambling debts. When Mr. Allan refused to pay them, Poe was forced to leave the University.

He enlisted in the U.S. Army in 1827 and entered the U.S. Military Academy at West Point, N.Y. He excelled in the study of languages but was expelled in 1831 for neglecting his duties. At this time Mr. Allan disowned him. Hire entire life Poe behaved erratically, making it difficult for him to hold down a steady job.

Some of his well-known poems are "The Raven" and "Annabel Lee." He published many short stories as well as poems. "The Cask of Amontillado," "The Gold Bug," and "The Fall of the House of Usher" are well-known short stories written by Poe. "The Murders in the Rue Morgue" is considered to be the first modern detective story.

He died in 1849 at the age of forty after several years of poor health. He suffered from periodic alcoholism complicated by drug use.

Edgar Allan Poe

The Best of Poe

The Pit and the Pendulum . . . . .9 – 16

The Fall of the House of Usher. . . . . .17 – 26

The Cask of Amontillado . . . . .27 – 32

The Murders in the Rue Morgue . . . . .33 – 63

The Pit and the Pendulum

In a dream—a nightmare—I saw the lips of the black-robed judges as they sentenced me to death. But first I would go to prison. I fainted from fear.

There were shadow memories of tall figures that lifted and carried me down....

At length I came to. I lay on my back in the dark. My hands were no longer tied.

Without opening my eyes I reached out my hand. It lay upon something damp and hard.

I was afraid to open my eyes, afraid that I would see—nothing! I tried, and it was so! There was only the dark.

I leaped to my feet and reached wildly in all directions. I was afraid I would feel the walls of a tomb!

At length my hands found a wall, smooth, slimy, and cold. I walked around it trying to figure out the size of my prison.

The ground was slippery. Soon I stumbled and fell.

Too tired to get up again, I remained there and fell asleep.

Awakening, I felt bread and water beside me. I ate and drank eagerly. Then I decided to explore further. I would try to cross my prison.

I stepped out carefully at first, then more freely. Suddenly I stumbled on the torn hem of my robe and fell forward.

I lay on my face. My chin rested on the prison floor. But from my lips up, my head touched nothing!

I put forward my arm, and trembled to find that I had fallen at the edge of a circular pit.

A piece of stone fell into the pit. For seconds I heard it echo far, far below.

Shaking all over, I felt my way back to the wall. Finally I fell into a heavy sleep. When I awoke, everything had changed.

A light came from somewhere above me, and I raised my head to look around. Frightening figures were painted on the walls. The circular pit lay in the exact center of my prison.

Above me on the high ceiling was painted a figure of old Father Time, with a clock's pendulum in place of his scythe.

Was the pendulum, as I first thought, part of the painting? Or did it really move?

A slight noise made me turn my head. Looking at the floor, I saw troops of large rats coming from the pit. They were after some meat that had been left beside me.

When I looked up again, the pendulum was swinging wider—and it had come closer to me!

At its end was a half-circle of steel—like a giant razor blade!

For hours—perhaps days—I watched in terror as it swung above me:

closer...

and closer...

...and yet closer.

And then, almost too late, I began to think. I reached for the remains of the meat and rubbed the straps that were holding me. Then I lay still.

The rats leaped in hundreds upon me and chewed at the straps.

Just as the blade began to cut through my robe, I felt the straps loosen. Carefully I rolled away and off the platform. I was free!

Then the pendulum stopped. It was drawn up to the ceiling. But the metal walls began to glow with heat!

My prison grew terribly hot—and the walls began to close in on me!

I gasped for breath. The burning walls pressed me toward the pit.

Moments later, I trembled on its edge. I was lost. I gave one loud, long, and final scream of terror.

Suddenly there was a loud blast as of many trumpets. With a harsh, grating sound, the walls rushed back. An arm caught mine as I began to fall, fainting, into the pit.

It was the arm of General Lasalle. The French army had entered Toledo. My enemies had been overthrown, and I was safe at last!

THE END

The Fall of the House of Usher

The Narrator

Roderick Usher

Madeline Usher

During the whole dark autumn day I had been riding alone through the dreary countryside. I found myself, at evening, near the gloomy old House of Usher. As soon as I saw it, my spirit was struck with sorrow.

18

I had come here because of a letter which had reached me a short time before.

Ah! From my old friend Roderick Usher, whom I have not seen for many years!

He suffers from a great illness and a mental problem as well. He wishes my company, as his oldest friend, to cheer him...

There is only one answer. I must go to him at once!

So it was that I came to the House of Usher.

A servant took my horse, and I entered the archway of the hall.

Another servant led me in silence through many dark hallways.

On a staircase we met the family doctor. I did not like his look of fear.

Then the servant led me into a large room where his master rose from a couch to greet me.

Roderick!

Ah, my good friend! How delightful to see you!

I gazed at my friend with sorrow at his changed appearance as he told me of his illness.

My senses are much too sharp. I can eat the most tasteless food, wear only the softest garments. The smells of flowers are too sweet to bear, and most sounds fill me with horror!

Most of all I fear... not danger...but the slightest thing which will upset my soul! Sooner or later I will lose life and reason altogether, fighting fear itself!

But much of his sorrow could be traced to the terrible illness of his beloved sister, who was slowly dying.

She has been my only companion for years. Her death will make me the last of the Ushers!

Her sickness has greatly puzzled the doctors.

She is wasting away to skin and bones... she can hardly move... she has seizures.

As he spoke, the lady Madeline passed through a far corner of the room without noticing me, and disappeared.

The sight could well have been that last I saw of her, for that night the illness forced her to bed.

For several days I tried to make my friend happy again.

We painted together.

We read together.

Sometimes I listened to him play the guitar.

Then one evening he told me suddenly that the lady Madeline had died.

I want to keep her body for two weeks in one of the vaults below the house. Later I will bury her in the family graveyard. My friend, will you help me?

Of course, Roderick! Anything!

We carried the body to a vault deep beneath the cellars of the house.

Our torches kept going out because there was so little air in the passageway.

Looking upon her face for the last time, I noted that she seemed almost alive. People with her illness, I knew, often looked like that even after death.

We were twins. Each of us always knew what the other was thinking.

Then we replaced the coffin lid and fastened it tightly.

The great iron door scraped on its hinges as we closed and locked it.

Days of sorrow brought changes in my friend. He roamed from room to room as if he were lost. He stared into space for long hours, as if listening to some sound that was not there.

I felt myself grow frightened at his terror. One night I rose, dressed, and paced the floor, unable to sleep.

It is only this dark room—and the storm outside that keep me from sleeping!

There was a light tap at the door, and Roderick entered. He was very upset.

Come, sit down! I shall read from one of your favorite books, and we will pass away this terrible night together!

In the story, the hero broke into a room: "He so cracked, and ripped, and tore...that the noise of the dry wood echoed..."

You heard?

It is nothing! The storm!

From below there came a scraping sound...and then a hollow clanging.

"...a great and terrible ringing sound..."

Yet from a distant part of the building, there had come a cracking, ripping noise.

Yes, I hear it! For hours, for days I've heard it— yet I dared not speak!

We have put my sister in her tomb alive!

I heard her first small movements in the coffin, scraping of the iron hinges, and now her footstep on the stair. I tell you that she now stands outside the door!

The heavy doors drew back—and there stood the figure of the lady Madeline of Usher, with blood upon her robes.

With a low, moaning cry, she fell upon her brother. Dying for certain now, she threw him to the floor with the weight of her body. And he, struck with terror, died beside her.

I fled from the house, out across the bridge and into the storm.

Suddenly behind me there shone a bright light.

It was a blood-red moon, shining through the widening crack in the house.

While I watched, the mighty walls split in two. And finally the pool at my feet closed over the remains of the House of Usher.

THE END

The Cask of Amontillado

Fortunato had harmed me a thousand times. But when he insulted me also, I swore to get even with him. I would kill him—and I would get away with it! Meanwhile, I let him think he was my good friend.

Ah, Fortunato!

Montresor, my dear friend!

One evening during the madness of the carnival season I met him on the street.

Montresor

Fortunato

Above all things, Fortunato considered himself a great judge of old wines. I would get back at him by using a barrel of Amontillado.

How lucky I met you! I have bought a cask of what passes for Amontillado, but I have my doubts.

Amontillado? A whole cask? And during the carnival? Impossible!

Amontillado!

I know. I should have spoken to you first. But you were not to be found, and I did not want to miss a great bargain!

I am on my way to Luchesi. He knows wines. He will tell me...

Luchesi cannot tell Amontillado from very poor sherry!

Come, let us go to your house. I will check this wine myself!

No, no! I don't want to take up your time.

You have a bad cold, and the vaults are very damp.

The cold is nothing! Amontillado! Let us go!

I allowed him to hurry me to my house.

This place is empty. The servants are all at the carnival.

Taking torches from their holders, we passed down a long, winding staircase into the catacombs of the Montresors. My friend's steps were unsteady from drink.

Steady, my friend! Don't slip.

The Amontillado! I can hardly believe it!

Soon a coughing spell forced Fortunato to stop.

Come, we must go back! The cold is bad for your cough.

Cough! Cough!

Your health is important! You are rich, respected, admired. You will be ill....

The cough is nothing! I shall not die of a cough!

Taking a bottle of wine from a rack nearby, I knocked off the neck and offered it to Fortunato. He drank eagerly.

True! And a drink of this wine will protect us from the damp!

He took my arm and we walked on, passing through low arches. At last we reached a deep cave with air so bad that our torches would hardly burn.

Three sides were lined with bodies. From the fourth, the bones had been thrown down and lay upon the earth.

Go ahead! The Amontillado is in there!

He stepped forward, but stopped at the rock wall. In it were two iron hooks, a chain, and a padlock. In a second I had wrapped the chain around his waist and fastened him there.

Pass your hand over the wall. It is very damp. If you don't want to go back, then I must leave you!

The Amontillado!

Digging into the pile of bones, I took out building stones, cement, and a trowel. Then I began to wall up the entrance to the cave.

There was a low, moaning cry from inside and a great rattling of chains. I sat down and waited.

Ahhhhhhh! Montresor! Montresor!

At last the clanking stopped. I continued my work. Finally there was only one stone to be fitted. There came from the cave a low laugh and a sad voice.

Ha! Ha! Ha! A very good joke indeed! We will have many a laugh about it at the carnival, over our wine....

The Amontillado?

Ha! Ha! Yes, the Amontillado. But is it not getting late? Will they not be waiting for us, Lady Fortunato and the rest? Let us be gone.

Yes, let us be gone.

FOR THE LOVE OF HEAVEN, MONTRESOR!

Yes, Fortunato.

There was no answer. I forced the last stone into its place. I plastered it up. Against the new wall I piled the old bones.

For half a century, no one has disturbed them.

The End

The Murders in the Rue Morgue

This was the scene of the murders in which the Paris police found themselves without a clue. My friend Dupin would solve the case by using his reason alone.

The Narrator

Dupin

French Sailor

Living in Paris in the spring of 1800, I visited a book shop one day in search of a special title.

Ah, monsieur...it is very rare and hard to find. I regret I do not have it!

This gentleman has just asked for the same book!

C. Auguste Dupin, monsieur, at your service.

I am happy to meet you, sir. Perhaps we should get together for our search.

So it was that Dupin and I became friends.

We found many interests in common. At last we moved into an apartment together in an old house on the Faubourg St. Germain. It was here that we first read of the murders in the Rue Morgue.

You read about the strange affair in the Rue Morgue?

A murder, wasn't it?

Murder, yes, but not of the usual kind.

Come! Picture this, if you will! About three o'clock this morning, the neighbors were awakened by terrible cries from the fourth floor of a house in the Rue Morgue...

Awful sounds, they were...like someone being killed!

Who lives there?

Madame L'Espanaye and her daughter Camille!

When no one answered the bell, the door was broken open.

Easy! That does it!

The cries has stopped. But as the men rushed up the first flight of stairs, they heard a new sound.

Listen!

It sounds like two men arguing!

But the sounds stopped, and all was quiet. The men ran through the house, searching from room to room. At last they came to a large back room on the fourth floor.

Locked—from the inside!

We must break it down.

The room was a terrible mess. The furniture was broken and thrown about.

What has happened?

There is no one here!

But where are the ladies?

A bloody razor!

Locks of gray—gray human hair—covered with blood!

A policeman picked up two bags from the floor.

Gold! At least four thousand francs in gold!

A safe—but open!

Nothing here but a few old letters.

But Madame L'Espanaye and her daughter! Where are they?

A great deal of soot seems to have been knocked down in the fireplace....

Do you think... oh, no!

Yes...it is here. A body!

The body was dragged out and examined.

She is cut and scratched, no doubt from the chimney. But it seems she has been choked to death.

The body of the daughter had been forced up the narrow chimney opening. It was still quite warm.

After searching the rest of the house without finding anything else, the group made its way into a small paved yard in the rear.

It is the old lady—Madame L'Espanaye!

But who could know her now!

Madame had been badly beaten. Her throat had been so deeply cut that her head was almost separated from her body.

To this terrible murder there is not yet the smallest clue.

We looked eagerly for the next day's newspapers. Though nothing had been found, an account was given of the people who had been questioned.

There was Pauline Dubourg, a washerwoman.

Yes, I am Pauline Dubourg. I have washed clothes for the L'Espanayes for three years.

I used to pick up the clothes and bring them to my home to wash.

How did the mother and daughter get along together?

Why, very well! They always seemed very kind to each other.

Did you ever see any other person in the house?

Never at all! There was no servant, and I never saw a visitor.

Were they well off? Did they have money?

They paid me well, that is all I know! As for what people say, Madame was thought to have some money saved up. I believe she told fortunes for a living.

Very well. We will write out what you have said. Please come to the station to sign it.

Goodbye, monsieur.

Also questioned was Pierre Moreau, a seller of tobacco.

All my life I have lived in the area, yes. Madame L'Espanaye has bought small amounts of tobacco from me for perhaps four years.

Madame owned the house, and they say she had money.

They also say the old lady told fortunes. But I don't believe it.

And why not?

They lived in a very quiet life. I have hardly seen anyone enter the door but the old lady and her daughter. A person came once or twice to deliver packages, and eight or ten times a doctor came.

Yes, I see.

It seems that many other neighbors said the same thing: that no one ever came to the house.

The shutters of the front windows were seldom open. Those in the rear were always closed, except for the one large back room on the fourth floor.

Isadore Muset, the policeman who first entered the house, made his report.

After breaking into the house, I led the way upstairs. Upon reaching the first landing, I heard two voices, loud and angry...

One was gruff, the other high and thin— a very strange voice!

The first voice was that of a Frenchman. The second was that of a foreigner—man or woman, I could not tell. I believe the language was Spanish.

Henri Duval, a neighbor who entered the house, agreed with Muset except about the voices.

The higher voice, man or woman I don't know. But I think the person spoke Italian.

It was not Madame L'Espanaye or her daughter?

No, no! It was not French, and it was not L'Espanayes! I have spoken with them many times!

A Dutchman passing by had joined the search of the house. Not speaking French, he was questioned in Dutch.

Monsieur Odenheimer agrees with the other reports except about the voices. He says the high voice was that of a man—a Frenchman!

William Bird, an Englishman who had lived for two years in Paris, had also passed by and joined the search. He was one of the first up the stairs.

The higher voice was very loud. It was certainly not that of an Englishman. It seemed to me to be German, but man or woman, I could not tell.

Monsieur Bird speaks German?

No, not at all.

Also questioned was Alfonzo Garcio, a Spanish undertaker who lived in the Rue Morgue.

I entered the house but I did not go up the stairs. I am too nervous! You understand?

But you could hear the voices?

Oh, yes, very well! The high voice was that of an Englishman. Of this I am sure!

You speak English, sir?

No, no! I judged by the kind of sound.

Alberto Montani, seller of candy, was also one of the first to go up the stairs.

The high voice? It was quick and uneven. I think it was the voice of a Russian.

Do you know Russian?

No, monsieur. I am an Italian. I have never spoken with a native of Russia!

Jules Mignaud, a banker of the firm of Mignaud et Fils, also spoke to the police.

About Madame L'Espanaye, monsieur...

Madame L'Espanaye opened an account eight years ago. She owned some property.

She took nothing out until three days before her death, when she came for the sum of 4,000 francs.

This sum was paid in gold, and a clerk took her home with the money.

May I talk with the clerk?

Certainly! Send in Le Bon!

Yes, I am Adolphe Le Bon. I went with Madame L'Espanaye and carried the two bags of gold to her home.

Did you enter the house?

No, monsieur. Her daughter met us at the door and took one of the bags, while the old lady took the other. I then bowed and left.

Now think carefully. Was there anyone else in sight— anyone going by?

There was no one at all! It is a side street, and very lonely.

Paul Dumas, a male doctor, also made a report.

I was called in about dawn to view the bodies. That of the the young lady was much cut and scraped. That it had been forced up into the chimeny would account for it.

There were deep scratches below the chin, with a series of spots which must have been the marks of fingers.

I think that Mademoiselle L'Espanaye was strangled to death.

The body of the mother was terribly cut up. The bones on the right side were nearly all broken. The whole body was discolored.

A heavy club, a bar of iron, a chair: such a weapon in the hands of a strong man might have given such results. No woman could have done it.

Besides that, the throat had been cut with something sharp, probably with a razor.

I see. Thank you, doctor.

The paper says that a murder so strange has never before been committed in Paris! There is not the shadow of a clue...

So who can solve it?

Later, the evening paper brought the news that although there were no new clues, Adolphe Le Bon had been arrested.

Let us check into these murders ourselves! Le Bon helped me once, for which I am grateful.

We will go and see the house with our own eyes. I know the chief of police, and shall have no trouble being allowed to do so.

Very well.

We reached the Rue Morgue in the late afternoon. There were still many people looking up at the house.

We walked through an alley and came to the rear of the house. Dupin looked around with great interest.

Ah!

Returning to the front door, we were let in by the police. We went up to the bedroom where the bodies still lay. Dupin looked at everything, including the bodies.

H'm....

On the way home we stopped at the offices of Le Monde, a daily paper read by sailors and ships' captains.

Wait for me. I'll be only a moment.

LE MONDE

Upon reaching home, Dupin would not talk about the murders until noon the next day. Then he made a surprising remark.

The police find this case hard to solve because it is so strange. But that very thing will lead me—or has already led me—to solve it!

I am waiting for a person who must have known about these crimes. I look for the man here—in the room—any moment now.

If he comes, we must keep him here. Here are some guns. We both know how to use them.

Scarcely believing what I heard, I took the gun, and Dupin continued.

There was the report of the two voices heard in argument. What was the strangest part of that report?

Everyone agreed that one man was a Frenchman. But everyone disagreed on the second, or higher voice.

Not only did they disagree, but each of these men, from five different countries, thought that voice spoke a foreign language!

Not a single word could be understood! This gives us a great clue!

Then—the room. The doors were locked from inside; there were no secret exits. The chimneys were too narrow to let a cat through. The killers must have left through the windows!

But the police found them nailed shut— from the inside!

They found that they could not force the windows up. There was a large nail through the window frame and sill of each one.

Well?

But I removed the nail, and I still could not force the window up! I looked for, and found, a hidden spring keeping it shut.

In the case of the window behind the bed, some years ago, the nail had been broken in two. Although it remained in place and looked whole, it no longer held the window shut.

If someone got away through that window, and let it close behind him, the hidden spring would lock the window. Yet it would seem that the nail was doing so!

So you have solved that part of it! But how did the killer get down?

A killer who was a good climber could have the outside shutter to swing himself from the window to the lightning rod. It runs from the roof to the ground nearby. He could have climbed down the rod!

So we have a killer with a strange voice who is a good climber. He also has great strength and is stupid enough to leave four thousand francs in gold behind him!

He is a madman! Someone who has escaped from a mental hospital!

Look at the lock of hair which I removed from Madame L'Espanaye's fingers!

I removed the hair from the envelope and looked at it carefully.

Dupin! This is not a human hair!

I did not say it was. Now read from this book.

It describes the large orang-utang ape of the East Indian islands. The animal had great size, strength, and agility. I understood the full story of the murders at last.

Yes, I see. But what of the second voice, the Frenchman?

I suppose him to be a sailor, the owner of the animal. He must know something of the murders.

Perhaps it got away from him and he followed it. It is probably still loose. I left this advertisement at the newspaper last night. I think it will bring him here.

it was a large orang-utang, the owner, (ascertained to be a sailor from a Maltese vessel) may have the animal again upon identifying it and paying a few charges,

At this moment we heard a step upon the stairs.

Be ready with your gun, but do not show or use it unless I tell you to.

Good evening.

Come in! Sit down! I suppose you've come about the orang-utang?

A fine animal—I envy you! How old is he?

I have no way of telling—four or five years, perhaps. You have him here?

Oh, no. He is at a stable nearby.

I don't want you to go through this for nothing. I'm very willing to pay a reward.

My reward shall be this. You shall tell me all you know about the murders in the Rue Morgue!

My friend, we mean you no harm. I know you did not kill those women. But an innocent man is now in jail. He is charged with a crime of which you can point out the killer!

So help me, I will tell you all I know. I am innocent of this crime!

He told us that he had brought the animal home from a recent voyage. He had kept it safely at his Paris home until it recovered from a foot wound. Then he planned to sell it. It was kept in a cage in an open closet.

But coming home late one night, he found the animal in his bedroom. It was imitating its master shaving!

Terrified at seeing the animal holding a razor, the sailor brought out a whip he sometimes used to control it.

But seeing the whip, the animal sprang through the door of the room, ran down the stairs, and jumped through an open window into the street.

Still carrying the razor, the ape led the sailor on a chase through the empty city streets. At last, seeing a lighted window, it rushed into a back yard in the Rue Morgue.

Catching sight of a lightning rod, it climbed it.

Reaching the fourth floor, it grasped a shutter and swung itself over and through the window.

The sailor climbed the rod easily, but as he did so, terrible screams came from the room. He could not reach the window, but could only look in.

Angered by her screams, the ape swept the razor across the old lady's throat.

Then, its anger made worse by the sight of blood, the ape grabbed the daughter, who had fainted, and choked her.

At this point, hearing the shouts of its owner, and looking up to see his face through the window, the ape's anger turned to fear. It rushed around the room knocking things over and breaking the furniture.

As if to hide what it had done, it thrust the body of the daughter up the chimney. Then it threw the old lady's body out the window.

The sailor quickly slid down the rod.

Terrified at what he had seen, he ran home, leaving the orang-utang to its fate. The ape must have left the room just before the door was broken in.

The next day we heard that the orang-utang had been caught. Its owner then sold it for a good sum.

When we told our story to the chief of police, Le Bon was let go at once.

You are free to go, Monsieur Le Bon.

A thousand thanks, Monsieur Dupin!

It was nothing at all.

The chief made a few remarks about the need for people to mind their own business, but Dupin said nothing.

Let him talk. It will make him feel better. I am happy that I solved the case before he could do so!

The END